P9-DBO-351
My Family
Me
Oliver
Moon
Dad
Mom
my sister, the Witch Baby

Oliver Moon and the Broomstick Battle

Sue Mongredien

Illustrated by

Jan McCafferty

For Daniel Brothwell, with lots of love

First published in 2007 by Usborne Publishing Ltd., Usborne House,
83-85 Saffron Hill, London EC1N 8RT, England. www.usborne.com

A CIP catalogue record for this book is available from the British Library.

UK ISBN 9780746084809 First published in America in 2011 AE.

American ISBN 9780794530389 JFMAMJJAS ND/10 01316/1

Printed in Yeovil, Somerset, UK.

Contents

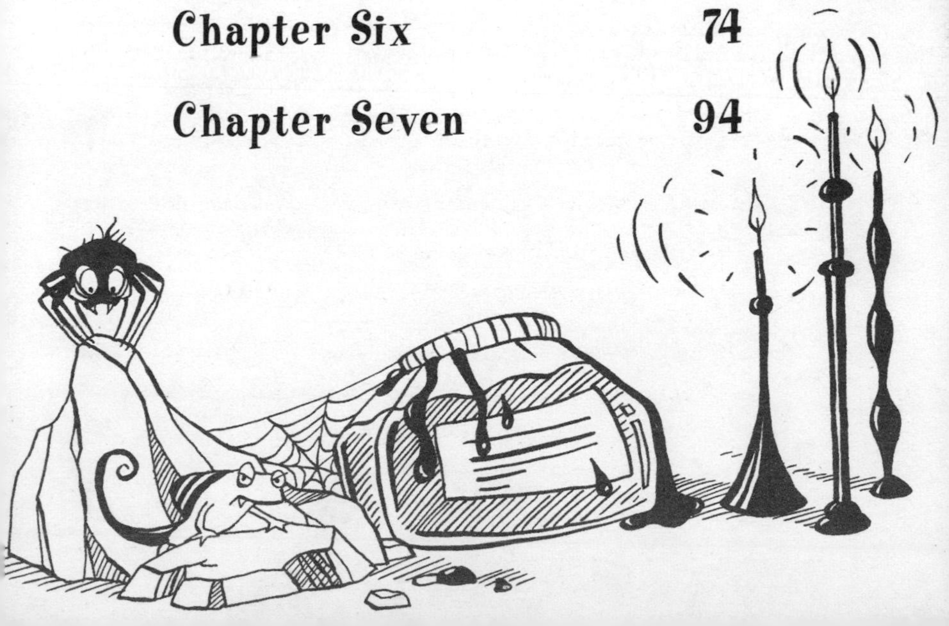

Oliver Moon was getting ready for bed. He had brushed his teeth with teeth-rotter paste. He had washed his face with skunk-whiff soap. He was just pulling on his toad-patterned pajamas, ready to climb into his spiderweb hammock, when he suddenly heard a lot of noise downstairs.

First, there came a high-pitched whizzing sound. Next, a loud voice he didn't recognize. And then a noise that sounded like fireworks going off, followed by an excited squeal from his mom. What was going on?

Oliver crept out of his bedroom to listen on the stairs.

"I can't wait! It's going to be fantastic!" he heard his dad cry.

Oliver's ears pricked up. *What* couldn't his dad wait for? *What* was going to be fantastic?

"Ooh, look!" he could hear his mom saying now. "Look at that!"

Then there came a wail from his little sister's room. "Too noisy! Me wake up!" the Witch Baby shouted.

Oliver went in to see her and carefully lifted her out of her crib. "Come on," he said, "we're going downstairs. Something exciting is happening, and we need to find out what!"

The Witch Baby gave a sniff. "Need to," she agreed, wriggling out of Oliver's arms and toddling ahead of him. "No more sleep. Finished sleep!"

Oliver and his sister went downstairs and peeped around the living room door. Mr. and Mrs. Moon were standing open-mouthed and staring at a...

Oliver rubbed his eyes. Was he *seeing* things?

He looked again. No, it was definitely there – a gigantic green witch's head, with no body, floating above the fireplace, and making some kind of announcement!

"Finally, there will be the Unicorn Showjumping event!" the witch's head declared. "Marvel as the unicorns fly over flaming fences! Gasp as they gallop over giant gates! Cheer as they chase through the enchanted slalom! All at this year's Cacklewick Olympics!"

Oliver watched in astonishment as the witch gave a wink, then vanished, with just a trace of green sparkly mist hanging in the air to show that she'd ever been there at all. A brightly colored leaflet shot out of the chimney and whirled all around the room before floating to the ground. "This was a public service announcement from Cacklewick Council," a different voice said. And then there was silence.

"Gone," the Witch Baby said, her eyes round with amazement. "Witch all gone!"

Mr. and Mrs. Moon turned at her words, looking surprised to see Oliver and his sister standing there in the doorway.

"Oops, sorry – did we wake you?" Mrs. Moon said, going over and scooping up the Witch Baby.

"Naughty Mommy," the Witch Baby told her reproachfully. "Too loud."

Mr. Moon was grinning at Oliver. "Did you catch any of that, Ol? Did you hear what the witch just said?"

"Only the bit about the unicorn race," Oliver said. "Is it really going to be the Cacklewick Olympics soon? I'd love to go!"

"Let's hope we can get tickets then!" Mr. Moon replied. He picked up the leaflet and sat down on the sofa with it. "Come on, let's take a look," he said, beckoning Oliver over.

Oliver didn't need asking twice! He was already really excited about the thought of the Olympics starting. He rushed to sit down next to his dad, leaning over to look at the leaflet.

There was a great long list of races and competitions, and Oliver skimmed through them eagerly. "Ooh! Boulder-Throwing for the giants," he read aloud. "That sounds good! Underwater Pearl Diving for the mermaids. And..." He broke off, as he saw a heading saying *Junior events*. "Hey," he said, "does this mean *I* can go in for something?"

His dad chuckled. "If you're picked, yes," he said. "Let's take a look. Junior events... Here we are. Olympic Slug-Eating. A Cauldron Chase. Oh yes, and the big one, of course – the Broomstick Obstacle Race."

Oliver's eyes lit up. He liked the sound of the Broomstick Obstacle Race! "I want to go in for that one," he said.

His dad grinned. "You and every other junior witch and wizard in Cacklewick, I bet," he said. "You won't remember the last Olympics, Ol, you were only a kid, but I'm pretty sure that was the one all the juniors wanted to win."

"Me race," the Witch Baby said, as she and Mrs. Moon came over to see.

Mr. Moon smiled at her. "You can enter one of the infant events, pickle," he said. "Let's see. There's the Toad-Dodging Toddle, or the Big Bat-Catch."

"Toads! Bats!" the Witch Baby

squeaked. "Me like! Yum yum!"

Mrs. Moon sat down to look at the leaflet. "What else is there? Ooh, Heavyweight Levitation, that sounds good," she said, pointing it out. "Competing wizards and witches have to try to lift the heaviest items possible – elephants, grand pianos, etc. – using only wand-power," she read aloud. "That will definitely be worth seeing. I remember at the last Olympics, Biceps Blackbeak lifted an entire family of trolls with his wand. It was quite a sight!"

Oliver wriggled excitedly on the sofa. "It *all* sounds good to me," he said, beaming. "I can't wait for it to begin!"

The very next day at Magic School, Mr. Goosepimple, Oliver's teacher, took attendance, then perched on the end of his desk to speak to the whole class.

"I'm sure everyone's heard about the Cacklewick Olympics by now," he said. "And I'm delighted to tell you that we will be putting forward Magic School students in all of the junior events, to compete against pupils from the Abracadabra Academy, and the School of Sorcery. Tryouts will be held on Friday, to select our team of athletes."

An excited buzz of whispers went around the classroom, and Oliver grinned at his best friend Jake Frogfreckle. How he hoped he and Jake would be picked to represent Magic School! Wouldn't that be fantastic?

"Now, let me explain about the actual events," Mr. Goosepimple went on. "There'll be an Olympic Slug-Eating contest – well, that speaks for itself. You have to eat as many slugs as you can within two minutes. Then there'll be a Cauldron Chase, which is a fun event –

you climb into a cauldron and chant a Running spell, so that it grows legs and can race against the other cauldrons."

He paused for breath, and Jake nudged Oliver. "That one sounds like fun," he whispered.

"Finally, there's the Broomstick Obstacle Race," Mr. Goosepimple said. "One for the daredevils! You'll be flying through, over and under a series of obstacles on your broomsticks. The obstacles will remain secret until the actual race, but in previous Olympic Games, contestants have flown through dark tunnels and enchanted forests, and have had to swerve around ogres and dragons. It's not one for the faint-hearted, believe me!"

Oliver felt really excited at his teacher's words. The Broomstick Obstacle Race sounded fantastic!

"So, let's start practicing," Mr. Goosepimple said, clapping his hands together and jumping off the desk. "Is anybody hungry?" He waved his wand and an enormous sack of squirming slugs appeared on the floor.

Oliver wrinkled his nose. He didn't much like eating slugs, although lots of his friends did.

Mr. Goosepimple picked up a stopwatch and looked around the class. "Who wants to go first?"

The slug-eating practice got under way. Mitch "the Mouth" Middlenight managed to scarf eighty-seven slugs in two minutes.

Carly Catstail did well, too, stuffing down seventy-nine slugs, and Eric Earwax ate seventy-five.

Oliver ate twelve – and that was twelve too many, he reckoned. He'd rather have a nice crunchy bat to snack on any day!

After that, they tried the Cauldron Chase. Mr. Goosepimple took them out to the playground where a line of huge iron cauldrons awaited them. He clambered into the nearest one, waved his wand and said, "Grow, legs, grow. Then go, legs, go!"

A flash of sparks swirled from the tip of his wand, and the cauldron jiggled around on its base. Then, with a tremendous squeaking, scraping kind of noise, the bottom of the cauldron started moving.

SQUEAK! Out kicked one leg.

SQUAWK! Out came a second leg.

The cauldron flexed both legs – and then, in the next instant, it was off, trotting across the playground at top speed. Oliver and Jake cracked up. It looked so funny!

"Your turn!" Mr. Goosepimple said, steering his cauldron back and motioning the class over to the other cauldrons.

Oliver stood in his and chanted the Running spell, then held tight to the cauldron as it tipped first one way then the other, while its legs grew. And then off he went, bumping over the ground in the cauldron as it galloped across the field. "Yahoo!" he cheered, trying to catch up with Jake's cauldron. "This is so cool!"

Not everybody got the spell exactly right. Pippi's cauldron only grew one leg, and toppled over with a clang. And Oliver was pleased to see that Bully

Bogeywort's cauldron only grew teeny-tiny legs that didn't take him anywhere fast. And poor old Mitch's cauldron ran in completely the wrong direction – and bashed straight into the school wall!

"That was awesome!" Jake said at the end of the race. His cauldron had run one of the fastest speeds and he patted it affectionately. "I loved it!"

Oliver clambered out of his cauldron. His legs felt very wobbly now that he was on solid ground again! "That was great," he agreed.

Mr. Goosepimple clapped his hands to get everyone's attention. "It's lunchtime now – make sure you have a good meal," he said. "You'll need every bit of energy for this afternoon because we'll be practicing the Broomstick Obstacle Race!"

"Cool," Oliver said, feeling tingly with excitement, as they headed for the cafeteria. "That's the one I'm looking forward to! I can't wait!"

Bully Bogeywort barged past Oliver just then, a mean smirk on his face. "Don't get your hopes up," he growled. "Because *I* want to be on the school team for the Obstacle Race – and nobody's going to stand in my way. Get it?"

Despite Bully's threats, Oliver could hardly eat his lunch because he was so excited about the practice session for the Broomstick Obstacle Race. What obstacles, he wondered, would Mr. Goosepimple have lined up for them? Dragons and ogres? Mountains to soar over? Burning tunnels to steer through?

Whatever their teacher had arranged, Oliver was sure it would be exciting and dangerous. He just knew it!

...Until he and his classmates got to the playing field after lunch, that was.

"Oh," Oliver said, looking around in surprise. There were no ogres or dragons to be seen. No high mountains or fiery tunnels. "Where are all the obstacles, then?"

Mr. Goosepimple looked a little embarrassed at the question. "Unfortunately," he said, "due to school budgets, I can't set up a lavish obstacle course for you every time we practice. Too costly, and too time-consuming, I'm afraid. Orders of Mrs. MacLizard."

"Oh-h-h-h," Pippi sighed. "That's no fun!"

"But we can still practice," Mr.

Goosepimple said, ignoring her. "So this is what we'll do. You can start by flying over to the tanglebranch trees, on the far side of the field, and slalom in and out of them. Then fly around the top tower of the school backward. And then..." He scratched his head thoughtfully. "Yes, and then you can swoop down over the frog pond and grab some hogweed. Everybody got that?"

"Yes, sir," chorused the class. Oliver swung a leg over his broomstick. So the practice run wasn't going to be *quite* as exciting as he'd thought...but it still sounded fun. And he still wanted to beat Bully Bogeywort, too!

"Everybody ready? Then your time starts...now. *Go!*" Mr. Goosepimple cried.

There was a rustling sound as the whole class took off into the air, their cloaks billowing behind them as they flew.

Like a flock of birds they all soared across the field to the tanglebranch trees. Oliver bent low over his broomstick, steering it carefully as he began the slalom.

In…out…in…out…

Oops, Colin Cockroach had caught his cloak on a prickly branch and was stuck.

In...out...in...out...

"Ouch!" yelped Hattie Toadtrumper as she flew too close to a nesting squabblehawk and it pecked her leg.

In...and...out again. Oliver had completed the tree slalom, but so had Bully Bogeywort, Pippi Prowlcat and... He gave a quick check over his shoulder. Ahh. So had most of the class. Oliver turned to face forward again and steered his broomstick toward the top tower of Magic School. Flying backward was tricky anyway, but flying backward with the rest of his class around him, all trying to get there first, was going to be even trickier!

Oliver took a deep breath and spun his broomstick around as he approached the tower. Bully Bogeywort spun his too, knocking Oliver's as he did and making him wobble dangerously. "Oops, sorry," Bully leered, looking positively gleeful and not sorry at all. "Careful there, Oliver, you almost fell off."

"He-e-e-elp!" came a cry just then and Oliver saw Carly Catstail bump into the wall of the tower, having turned too close. She toppled off her broomstick and crashed toward the ground.

Mr. Goosepimple only just managed to cast a spell in time to float her safely down to the grass.

Horace Hogbody had fallen, too. And Jake had somehow managed to fly through an open window of the tower, so he was out. There was only about half the class left in the race now.

Oliver was determined to make it to the end. This was only a practice run, after all – and if he couldn't complete this course, there was no hope for him as an Olympic contestant. He concentrated as hard as he could on getting around the tower backward without scraping his shins on the tower wall, or crashing into anybody else.

"Whoops!" wailed Lucy Lizardlegs just then, getting caught up in the school flag that fluttered from the tower. Another competitor out of the race…

Yes! Oliver had made it all the way around. Now he just had to swoop over the frog pond and gather some hogweed. No problem!

Oliver, Bully and Pippi were all neck and neck as they flew lower and lower, nearing the swampy pond.

And then, as Oliver let go of his broomstick with one hand, ready to snatch up a stalk of hogweed, Bully slammed his broomstick straight into Oliver's side.

SPLASH! Oliver tumbled head first into the pond, swallowing a whole lump of frogspawn as he did so.

He clambered out, dripping with pond water and slime, and scowled as Bully Bogeywort just beat Pippi back to where Mr. Goosepimple was standing, checking his stopwatch for their times.

"Well done, you two! Excellent racing!" Mr. Goosepimple cried, clapping his hands. He didn't seem to have noticed Bully's bit of cheating, Oliver thought crossly, as he sloshed along toward his teacher, muddy pond water squishing between his toes. "And third place for you, Oliver, well done," Mr. Goosepimple continued, as Oliver reached him. "Keep up the good work, all of you, and you might just get picked as Olympic racers!"

Oliver glared at Bully, but received only a smirk in response.

Other witches and wizards were straggling over to Mr. Goosepimple too. Colin had a big rip in his cloak where he'd torn it getting out of the tree, and Hattie was rubbing her leg where it had been pecked.

“Bad luck, you guys,” Mr. Goosepimple said, “but there’s still plenty of time to practice before the tryouts on Friday. You know what they say – practice makes perfect!”

Oliver wrung out his cloak, which was still very wet and slimy, and gritted his teeth. Practice makes perfect? All right, then. If it meant beating Bully to a place in the Olympic tryouts, then Oliver would happily practice as he’d never practiced anything before!

Oliver was still thinking about how to beat Bully when he got home. "I've got great news," his mom said, as soon as Oliver walked through the front door. "I was in town earlier with your sister and Potions R Us was running a free competition for all their shoppers. Guess the number of spiders in the witch's hat, it was."

“Spiders!” the Witch Baby chimed in, wiggling her fingers. “Spidery spidery spiders!”

Mrs. Moon beamed. “Yes, there were hundreds of them. Well, thousands actually. Two thousand, eight hundred and ninety-seven to be precise.”

Oliver looked up. “And you guessed it right?”

“Two thousand, eight hundred and ninety-*nine*, I said,” Oliver’s mom replied. “But it was the nearest answer…so I was the winner. And look what I won!” She held something out toward Oliver, and he looked closely at what lay in her hands.

Cacklewick Olympics…family pass?

A family pass! To the Olympic Games! No way!!

Oliver forgot about Bully Bogeywort. He blinked and stared at the bright green ticket in his mom's hands. "We're going to the Olympics?" he asked in delight. "We're really going?"

"Oh yes," his mom said, hugging him. "Free tickets, Oliver. To all the events!"

"Yesss!" Oliver cheered, dancing around

with his sister in excitement. "We're going to the Olympics! We're going to the Olympics!"

"Hooray!" yelled the Witch Baby, kicking her chubby legs in the air with glee. "Going to Limpics, hooray!"

The Moons celebrated that evening with take-out eye-pie and fries, and a bottle of fizzy swamp juice. Mrs. Moon had phoned Oliver's dad at work to tell him the news, and he'd arrived home with a special surprise, too. "An Image Catcher!" he announced proudly, getting it out from his cloak pocket. "Top of the line. We won't miss a thing!"

Mrs. Moon gasped at the sight of it, and her expression turned anxious.

"Aren't they very expensive?" she asked doubtfully.

Mr. Moon shrugged. "Well...a bit," he replied. "But think of all the money we've saved on tickets, with you winning the free pass! We'd have spent it anyway, and the Olympics are only on every five years..."

"How does it work?" Oliver asked eagerly, staring at the contraption.

"You look through here," Mr. Moon said, holding it up to his face and peering through the little window. "And you press this silver button here, and it catches images onto a film. Then you can watch it on your screen at home. Let me show you."

He switched on the Image Catcher and peered through it at Oliver and the Witch

Baby. "Go on," he said, "do something funny."

"La la la," sang the Witch Baby, skipping around. "Humpy Lumpy sat on a wall..."

"Hello," Oliver said, waving at the Image Catcher and feeling a bit shy.

"Okay, that'll do," Mr. Moon said, pressing a blue button on the machine. "Now all we do is turn on the TV..." He waved his wand at the wall, and a screen appeared. A witch was reading the local news in a solemn voice. "And then I flick this switch and..." Nothing happened. "Oops, sorry," said Mr. Moon. "I meant *this* switch..."

"Ooh!" gasped Mrs. Moon.

The witch had disappeared. And there in her place on the screen was a picture of the Moons' own living room, with the Witch Baby dancing around. "La la la, Humpy Lumpy sat on a wall," they heard her sing.

"That *me*!" the Witch Baby squealed, toddling over and prodding at herself on screen.

"And there's me!" Oliver laughed, his eyes wide as he saw himself waving and saying hello.

Mr. Moon looked as if he were about to burst with pride. "See? How good is that?" he said. "So we can catch all the best Olympic events on it, then watch them again, right here in our own home!"

Oliver went to bed that night and dreamed of winning the gold medal in the Broomstick Obstacle Race, and then watching it again and again at home. Oh, if only it would come true!

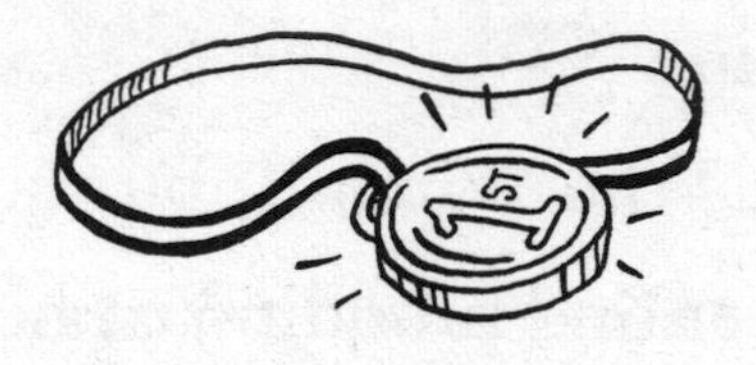

On Friday, Mrs. MacLizard, the head teacher, called a special school assembly. Once everyone was sitting down, she appeared onstage in a puff of smoke, her squinty black eyes twinkling as she smiled around the room. "Good morning, everyone!" she said. "I hope you've been having fun practicing all the

Olympic events?"

"Yes, Mrs. MacLizard," everyone chorused politely, Oliver included.

"Good," she said. "Because now we need to find out who wants to try out for each event! So...hats up if you've got a hearty appetite, and want to try out for the Slug-Eating contest."

There was a flurry of movement, as ten or so pointy hats were raised in the air. Oliver kept his hat firmly on his head.

"Thank you," Mrs. MacLizard said. "The Cauldron Chase, next. Hats up, please, all those who think they can make their cauldrons run the fastest!"

Jake thrust his hat up eagerly, along with several other witches and wizards, and Mrs. MacLizard smiled. "Excellent!"

she said. "And finally, hats up if you want to try out for the Broomstick Obstacle Race."

Oliver shot his hat up immediately along with a lot of other wizards and witches. Oliver glanced along his row to see Bully Bogeywort and Pippi Prowlcat both holding up their hats, too.

Bully caught Oliver looking at him and snarled back. "You've got no chance, Moon," he said. "Not against me, anyway!"

"Marvelous." Mrs. MacLizard beamed. "I'm sure you'll all have great fun taking part in the tryouts. And may the best witches and wizards win!"

Oliver flicked another sideways glance at Bully, who grinned nastily back at him. "You bet I will," Bully muttered.

Later that day, the tryouts got under way. To Oliver's dismay, the places on the school Olympic team for the first event were snapped up by the Magic School senior monitors. Okay, so they were older than Oliver and his friends and maybe it was to be expected. All the same, it was a blow to see Big Bertie Baines swallow a whole bucket of slugs in one mouthful, easily beating Mitch and Carly in the Slug-Eating challenge.

Then came the Cauldron Chase time trials. Jake had been training hard all week and Oliver gave a huge sigh of disappointment when his friend crossed the finish line in fourth place, just missing out on a place on the Olympic team.

Finally, after lunch, it was the Broomstick Obstacle Race tryout. Oliver, Bully and Pippi were taking part, of course, along with about ten other older witches and wizards. The rest of the school came out to watch on the field, where a whole series of obstacles had been magicked up.

"Whoa," Jake breathed, stopping dead. "A burning tower?"

"And is that a giantess?" Oliver asked, feeling nervous at the sight.

"It certainly is," Mrs. MacLizard said, overhearing them. "And a grouchy one at that. You'll have to fly well away from her, otherwise she might grab you." She cackled merrily. "Those massive fingers of hers could easily crush you to jelly!"

"Are you sure you still want to go in for this?" Jake asked Oliver under his breath.

Oliver hesitated for a second, then nodded. "I'll be all right," he said to Jake, trying to sound confident.

"So, to start with, you need to fly between the top turrets of the burning tower," Mrs. MacLizard announced. "There's a twenty-foot gap between them – plenty of room. Oh, and if your broomstick catches fire, you'll need to fly straight down to the frog pond and dunk yourself, all right?"

Millie Mildew, one of the Year Nine witches, let out a little whimper. "I don't like the sound of this," Oliver heard her mutter to her friend.

Pippi was looking rather pale, too. "If my cloak gets burned, my mom's going to go crazy," she said anxiously.

"Next, you'll need to dive down to the ground and collect a snake from the pit," Mrs. MacLizard said. "There's one for everybody, so don't be greedy and take two. Now, these are poisonous snakes, so be careful! Then, you need to fly back up into the air and release your snake into the tanglebranch tree over there," she went on. "Tap it twice with your wand and it should turn into a bluebird. If it turns into anything else, you're out of the race. Then, once you've flown around the giantess, you can head to the finish line."

Oliver picked up his broomstick and gripped the handle, looking at the burning tower with a jittery feeling inside. This was going to be much harder than he'd thought!

Then he saw Bully's mean yellow eyes checking him out. "Not scared, are you?" Bully sneered.

"Course not!" Oliver retorted, although that wasn't strictly true. "Why, are you?"

Bully laughed as if this was the funniest thing he'd heard all day. "Scared? Of that simple little stuff? Not likely," he said. "Bring it on!"

"The giantess will probably be scared of *him*," Pippi muttered to Oliver. "The horrible show-off!"

Mrs. MacLizard waved her wand and it made the sound of a horn. PARP!

"That will be your starting signal," she told them. "So if you're ready, kindly stand astride your broomsticks in takeoff position."

Oliver put one leg over his broomstick, his hands feeling clammy on its handle.

"On your mark," said Mrs. MacLizard, holding her wand in the air, "get set..."

PARP!

"Go!"

With a whoosh, all the contestants took off into the air. Oliver gripped his broomstick tightly and zoomed up higher and higher until he was level with the burning tower. *Whizz!* Concentrating hard, he flew right between the fiery turrets in as straight a line as he could manage.

"Help!" came Millie's voice somewhere behind him. Seconds later, she shot past him, her broomstick flaming, and nosedived into the frog pond with an almighty ka-sploosh.

Oliver zoomed toward a huge pit in the ground that was wriggling and squirming with snakes. Pippi was already there, grabbing a large yellow snake and whizzing off again. Oliver pointed the end of his broomstick downward and tried to catch up. But just as he reached the pit, Bully soared down next to him – and gave him a push that nearly sent Oliver flying into the mass of snakes!

"Hey!" Oliver cried, getting his balance just in time. "Watch it!"

Bully bared his teeth in a grin. "*You* watch it," he replied. "Watch me win, I mean!" And with that, he snatched up a fat red snake and flew off toward the tanglebranch tree.

Oliver was fuming. Bully Bogeywort always had to try and cheat! He reached down and picked up a pale blue snake, which flicked its forked tongue at him, and off he went again, chasing after the others.

Freddie Frogmouth, one of the older wizards, had reached the tanglebranch tree as well as Bully and a couple of witches, Sasha Slimeskin and Katie Crowfoot, when Oliver arrived. They were all trying to turn their snakes into bluebirds by tapping them with their wands.

Tap, tap. Freddie's snake turned into a rabbit and sat trembling on the branch.

"Freddie – you're out of the race!" they heard Mrs. MacLizard cry.

Tap, tap. Sasha's snake turned into a bluebird, and flapped away. So did Katie's. "Yes!" cheered Sasha, setting off toward the giantess, with Katie flying after her.

Tap, tap. Bully's snake turned into a bluebird, and flapped away. "Success!" Bully gloated, whizzing off at top speed.

Tap, tap. Oliver's snake turned into a bluebird, too. He was still in the race!

He zoomed toward the giantess. Sasha buzzed a little too close to her head, and the giantess slapped a huge meaty hand in the air, knocking Sasha off her broomstick onto a patch of springy grass. Bully and Oliver both flew a safe distance from her without any trouble – so now there was just the finish line to race for!

There were only the three of them left in it. The frog pond had about four wet witches and wizards clambering out of it.

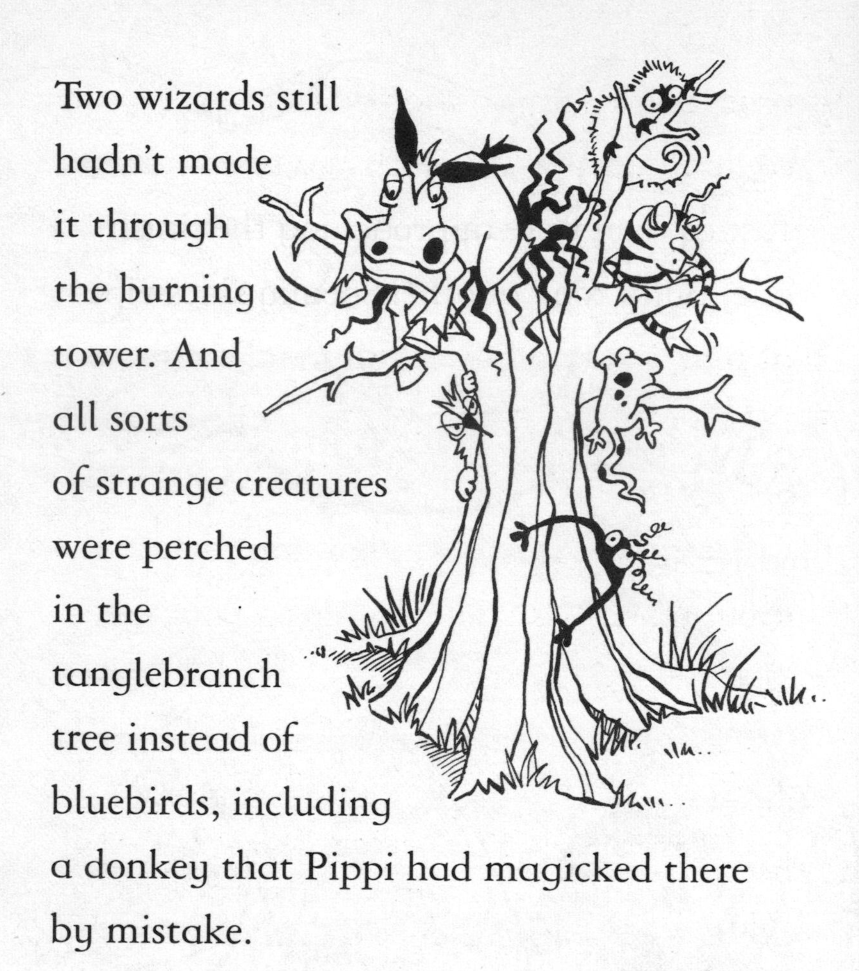

Two wizards still hadn't made it through the burning tower. And all sorts of strange creatures were perched in the tanglebranch tree instead of bluebirds, including a donkey that Pippi had magicked there by mistake.

Oliver, Bully and Katie were all level now – yet Oliver knew that only the fastest two would get on the Magic School Olympic team. Oliver was low over his broomstick, urging it on as fast as he could make it go. And then.... boomph! Just as they were approaching the finish line, Bully took another sneaky sideswipe at him, sending Oliver flying off course.

"Yippeee!" screamed Katie, whizzing over the line.

"Yesssss!" roared Bully, flying to the ground and punching the air in triumph. "I am the champion!"

"Champion *cheat*, you mean," Oliver said, floating down to land and glaring at him. He couldn't believe that none of the teachers seemed to have noticed Bully's cheating!

Bully shrugged. "Who cares? I'm on the team – and you're not," he said. "Face it, Moon. You're a *loser*."

Oliver felt miserable the whole next week. He'd been picked as a reserve for the team, but that made him feel as if he was having his nose rubbed in it, training with the actual team members. And, of course, Bully Bogeywort didn't stop gloating.

"Ignore him," Mrs. Moon said, when

Oliver trudged home at the end of the week. "Cheats always get their comeuppance. And anyway, being a reserve is fantastic! You'll get to see everything behind the scenes. You've done wonderfully, Oliver. We know that – and we're really proud of you."

"Thanks, Mom." Oliver sighed.

"And it's the start of the Olympics tomorrow," his dad said. "We'll have a great time, you wait."

As the Moon family arrived at the Olympic stadium the next day, Oliver couldn't stop smiling. "Wow," he breathed, gazing up at the huge arena that had magically appeared just outside Cacklewick.

There were hundreds of witches and wizards milling around, some selling programs and souvenirs, others with autograph books and Image Catchers. Giants were tramping in to compete in the Boulder-Throwing event, the sky was

black with incoming broomsticks, and Oliver was sure he spotted a unicorn galloping through the clouds, too. "This is so exciting!" he said. "I can't believe we're actually here!"

"Hooray for Limpics!" his sister

cheered, staring around with bright eyes.

But then Oliver remembered that he wasn't actually going to be competing. Oh yeah, and Bully Bogeywort was on the team, not him. The smile slipped off his face at once. It was so unfair!

Oliver and his family joined a line to get into the arena. Once inside, he gasped. Powerful magic had been cast so that the inside of the arena seemed as big as the city outside, with a lake for the mer-people to race in, a vast field for the giants, a stretch of sky roped off for the Mid-Air Bowling competition, and the main Broomsticking racetrack in the center of it all.

"Me toddle now?" the Witch Baby asked, gazing around. "In lake?"

"No, pumpkin, not in the lake," Mrs. Moon replied, hugging her. "But you're right – we need to find where your race is." She checked her witch-watch. "Oliver, you have to check in with your team, don't you?"

"I can take him," Mr. Moon said. "Shall we meet you for the Strongwizard contest in half an hour?"

Mrs. Moon nodded. "See you later."

Oliver and his dad made their way toward the locker room, Mr. Moon with his eye glued to his Image Catcher, recording everything in sight. They passed a group of witches giving their snakes some last-minute advice before the Big Slither race, some baby dragons drinking gasoline in preparation for the

Fire-Breathing event, and a team of wizards flexing their muscles before the Strongwizard contest.

There were big screens everywhere, showing what was happening around the stadium, too. Oliver hardly knew what to look at next, there was so much to see.

In the locker room, Mrs. MacLizard

was giving a pep talk to all of the Magic School entrants. There was Katie, with her best cloak on, and speed-goggles, and...Oliver stared. Where was Bully? He wasn't there! He was missing!

Oliver double-checked the room. No. He definitely wasn't there. Did this mean...? Could he possibly be *ill*?

Was he going to miss the race? Would Oliver have to step in and take his place?

"Where's Bully Bogeywort gone?" Mrs. MacLizard snapped just then, as if reading Oliver's thoughts. "I saw him just now but he seems to have vanished. I've called him a few times but he hasn't come. Has anybody seen him lately?"

The rest of the team shook their heads. "Maybe he's in the bathroom," Katie suggested.

Mrs. MacLizard tutted. "Well, that's all very well, but doesn't he know the race is starting soon? He needs to be getting ready!"

Oliver sighed. So Bully *wasn't* ill. He *had* turned up for the race. But if he didn't come back soon, he might well miss it...

That would be good! a little voice said in Oliver's head. *Then YOU might get asked to step in and take his place!*

Oliver frowned. But Bully had been picked to represent the school. And even though he cheated sometimes he was actually a good, fast racer, much as Oliver hated to admit it...

Oliver gritted his teeth and put up his hand. "I'll go and look for him if you like, Mrs. MacLizard," he said. Not because he liked Bully. And not because he wanted Bully to take part in the race. He would go and look for him for the good of Magic School. That was all.

Mrs. MacLizard smiled. "Would you, dear? That would be very helpful. Thank you," she said.

Oliver's dad patted him on the back. "I'm proud of you," he said as they left the room. "That was a big thing to do. You're a good sport, Ollie." He turned his attention to the Image Catcher. "Now," he said, fiddling with it. "While we're looking for Bully, I'll do a bit of backstage filming. I promised the neighbors I'd record everything on this so we can show them later."

Oliver and his dad went along the corridor into the next room, which was full of sporting equipment. There were piles of Air-Light bowling balls, cages for dangerous creatures, boulders for the giants and...Bully Bogeywort. Not in the bathroom, after all, but rubbing great dollops of Slipgrease all over a pile of broomsticks instead!

SLIPGREASE

Oliver pulled his dad behind a huge stack of boulders, not wanting Bully to see them. "What's he doing *here*?" Mr. Moon hissed, confused. He hadn't seen the big jar of Slipgrease. He hadn't seen the sneaky smile on Bully's face either.

Oliver put his finger to his lips. "He's cheating, that's what he's doing!" he whispered into his dad's ear.

Mr. Moon looked shocked at Oliver's words. "Cheating?" he mouthed, his eyes wide.

Oliver nodded, and then a great idea came to him. "Dad, will you record him?" he asked, pointing at the Image Catcher. "Then we can tell Mrs. MacLizard, and show her what Bully's been doing!"

Without another word, Mr. Moon lifted

the Image Catcher to his eye, pressed the silver button and leaned silently around the boulders to film Bully at work.

Oliver peeped around to watch too. He couldn't believe it. He knew Bully was a cheat, of course, he'd seen that much at Magic School. But to cheat in the Olympic Games was something else altogether.

"There," Bully said, when he'd put Slipgrease on all the broomstick handles except his own. He tipped on some Itching Powder too, for good measure, and grinned broadly. "And the gold medal goes to...Bully Bogeywort, thanks very much!" He laughed softly to himself. "This is going to be fun."

"Bully! Bully Bogeywort, where are you? Come on!" came Mrs. MacLizard's voice just then, and Bully wiped his greasy hands on his cloak. “The race starts in five minutes!”

“Coming!” Bully called, with another grin. Oliver and his dad pressed themselves into the side of a boulder as he went past, whistling.

"This is outrageous!" Mr. Moon exclaimed as soon as Bully was out of earshot. "We can't let the race go ahead!"

They hurried out of the room, past a big screen showing a group of mermaids doing a complicated dance routine in the lake.

But Mrs. MacLizard was nowhere to be seen. Just then Oliver spotted a wizard in a referee cloak. “Excuse me,” he said, waving and running over. “Can we just show you something?”

“Of course,” said the referee, and Mr. Moon folded out a tiny replay screen from the Image Catcher and jabbed at a button. Oliver gasped as the mermaids that had been on the big stadium screen vanished – and footage of the equipment room appeared up there, showing Bully Bogeywort up to his cheating tricks!

“Oh,” said Mr. Moon, frowning over the Image Catcher controls. “Oops, sorry, I didn’t mean that to happen…”

But a great shout had already gone up from the main arena – and Oliver realized that every single screen around the place was showing the footage of Bully Bogeywort. Wizards and witches everywhere were stopping whatever they were doing and staring at the action on the screens. "What's going on? What's he *doing*?" one witch cried, squinting at the picture. "Is that really Slipgrease he's putting on those broomsticks?"

"Who is he, anyway?" another witch asked, looking furious under her mane of long silver hair. "Isn't that against the rules?"

"There," Bully said on screen at that moment. "And the gold medal goes to...Bully Bogeywort, thanks very much!" He laughed. "This is going to be fun."

"Bully Bogeywort, eh?" the referee wizard boomed. "I think that young wizard just disqualified himself from the entire Olympic Games!"

Everything went a bit strange after that. Bully Bogeywort was sent home in disgrace – and, as the reserve, Oliver was called up to take his place in the Broomstick Obstacle Race!

The race was delayed while the broomsticks were thoroughly cleaned, and Oliver tried to calm his nerves by watching his sister in the Toad-Dodging Toddle. The toddlers were supposed to go across a field as fast as they could, dodging all the big yellow toads that were placed croaking everywhere, but the Witch Baby went straight up to the nearest one and sat down to give it a big cuddle. "Ahhh!" she cooed, tickling it under the chin. "Nice toad! Hooray for Limpics, toad!"

"Ribbet!" went the nice toad in surprise, looking rather squashed in her cuddle. "Ribbet!"

Oliver could hardly pay attention, though, because he couldn't stop thinking about his own race that was coming up. What obstacles would there be? Would the other racers be really, really fast? And what if he, Oliver, fell off his broomstick and let his school down in front of everyone?

Oliver tried to distract himself by going to watch the Strongwizard contest with his family, but barely even noticed Wizard Brickbreath lifting a double-decker bus with his little finger, or Witch Mighty-Muscles balancing a rhinoceros on her nose.

At last, it was time to take his place on the starting line with the other Obstacle Race contestants, and Oliver felt sick. There was Katie, of course, from Magic School, and ten other junior witches and wizards that he didn't know from rival schools in Cacklewick. The arena was plunged into darkness as the contestants lined up in their starting positions. Oliver's heart pounded as he stood there, clutching his broomstick and wondering what lay ahead of him. He could still hardly believe that he was here at all, about to take part in an Olympic race!

PEEEEP!

A whistle blew – and then Oliver blinked, dazzled, as the arena floodlights came on again and the race began. He kicked off into the air at once, his mouth dry with nerves. There was an enormous troll straight ahead, swiping his gigantic hands through the air, and licking his lips. Oliver flew wide of him, just as the troll made a grab for one of the other wizards.

His heart pounded. Whew. Past the first obstacle. That was good. It would have been awful to get knocked out of the race before it had even really begun.

Oliver blinked as an enormous spider's web suddenly appeared in front of him without warning. One witch flew straight into it and got completely stuck, but Oliver steered his broomstick up as sharply as he could, and just managed to get over the top. He had passed the second obstacle – but it looked as if most of the others had, too.

He could see a group of screech-raptors circling in the sky ahead now. Oliver gulped. Screech-raptors were vicious, birdlike creatures with long beaks and sharp claws. They were very aggressive and would attack anything near them. Oh – and here they came, zooming toward him and the other contestants, making snapping noises with their beaks.

Oliver swerved to the side, trying to avoid them, but one of the raptors seemed to be making a beeline for him. "Shoo! Shoo!" he shouted, hoping to frighten it away, but the raptor only flapped its leathery wings harder, and squawked defiantly. It was getting closer by the second. It was so close he could almost feel its hot breath on him!

With every bit of strength he had, Oliver spun his broomstick around, so that it clipped the raptor sharply on the beak. "Caw!" the raptor yelped in a surprised sort of way, and dropped through the air away from him.

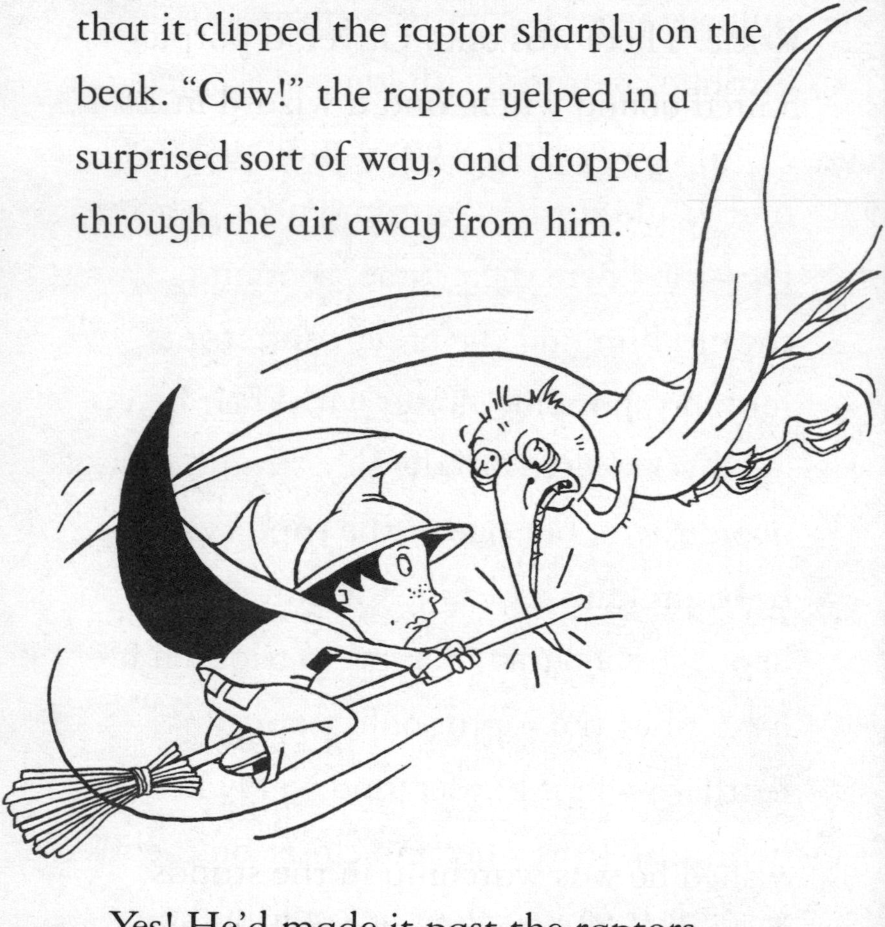

Yes! He'd made it past the raptors. With a quick glance over his shoulder,

Oliver saw that lots of the other racers were being chased off by them, including Katie. There was only Oliver, a purple-haired young witch, and a wizard in a red cloak left in the race now – with just one more obstacle to get past!

Oliver gulped as a fire-breathing green dragon appeared in the sky before him, smoke billowing from its nostrils. There was no way he was getting too close to *that,* he thought in horror. It would burn his broomstick to ash within seconds!

The dragon flapped its great wings and Oliver felt very scared. Part of him wished he was watching in the stands with the rest of his family. But the other, braver part of him knew he had to try to get past it. He'd made it this far, hadn't he? He *had* to keep going!

The red-cloaked wizard dodged to the left of the dragon, nimbly jumping a jet of flame. The dragon swished its tail crossly, and the crowd cheered.

The purple-haired witch dived below the dragon, daringly skimming its underbelly as she flew. The dragon pawed at the air in rage, and the crowd stamped their feet in excitement.

And Oliver took a deep breath and steered his broomstick up, up and over the dragon's head, his heart hammering as if it were going to burst. Just at the last moment, the dragon looked up, its pale eyes fixed on Oliver, and Oliver gave a shout of terror as it opened its mouth...

With a last desperate burst of energy, Oliver pushed himself forward and away from the dragon, just as the hot flames streamed from its mouth. Oliver felt the heat right behind him, but managed to avoid the fiery breath, with only the very tips of his broomstick getting singed.

He'd done it! And the finish line was in sight!

Oliver hunched low over his broomstick, urging it on. He was almost there!

The red-cloaked wizard whizzed over the finish line. "Gold!" called the referee.

The purple-haired witch zoomed over just behind him. "Silver!" announced the referee.

And Oliver, feeling faint with excitement, soared over in third place. "Bronze!" cried the referee.

And then crowds of people were running over – his mom and dad with the Witch Baby, and Jake, and Katie, and Mr. Goosepimple and oh, so many others, all hugging him and patting him on the back and saying, "Well done!"

Oliver stood there, beaming with pride and happiness. He'd shown Bully Bogeywort he wasn't a loser, and had actually won a bronze medal at the Cacklewick Olympic Games to prove it!

"And it's all on here," his dad told him,

patting the Image Catcher. "So we can watch it over and over again at home. What a race. What a performance!"

"Thanks, Dad," Oliver said. He felt so happy, he couldn't stop smiling.

"Hooray for Limpics!" the Witch Baby cheered, giving Oliver a big wet kiss.

Oliver grinned at her. "You're right," he said. "Hooray for the Olympics!"

The End

Don't miss Oliver's fab website,
where you can find lots of fun, free stuff.
Log on now...

www.olivermoon.com

Oliver Moon Junior Wizard

Collect all of Oliver Moon's magical adventures!

Oliver Moon and the Potion Commotion
Can Oliver create a potion to win the Young Wizard of the Year award?

Oliver Moon and the Dragon Disaster
Oliver's sure his new pet dragon will liven up the Festival of Magic...

Oliver Moon and the Nipperbat Nightmare
Things go horribly wrong when Oliver gets to take care of the school pet.

Oliver Moon's Summer Howliday
Oliver suspects there is something odd about his hairy new friend, Wilf.

Oliver Moon's Christmas Cracker
Can a special present save Oliver's Christmas at horrible Aunt Wart's?

Oliver Moon and the Spell-off
Oliver must win a spell-off against clever Casper to avoid a scary forfeit.

Oliver Moon's Fangtastic Sleepover
Will Oliver survive a school sleepover in the haunted house museum?

Oliver Moon and the Broomstick Battle
Can Oliver beat Bully to win the Junior Wizards' Obstacle Race?

Happy Birthday, Oliver Moon
Will Oliver's birthday party be ruined when his invitations go astray?

Oliver Moon and the Spider Spell
Oliver's Grow-bigger spell lands the Witch Baby's pet in huge trouble.

Oliver Moon and the Troll Trouble
Can Oliver save the show as the scary, stinky troll in the school play?

Oliver Moon and the Monster Mystery
Strange things start to happen when Oliver wins a monster raffle prize...